Classics for Beginning Readers™

Reader's Digest Young Families

The Country Mouse and The City Mouse

Designers: Elaine Lopez and Wendy Boccuzzi
Editors: Suzanne G. Beason and Sharon Yates
Editorial Director: Pamela Pia

Adapted text by Karen Jennings and Mark Pierce copyright © 2003 Reader's Digest Young Families, Inc.
Based on the original story written by Aesop.
Illustrations by Dennis Hockerman copyright © 2003 Reader's Digest Young Families, Inc.

Printed in China.

Classics for Beginning Readers ™

Reader's Digest Young Families

The Country Mouse and The City Mouse

Based on the fable written by

Aesop

Retold by Karen Jennings and Mark Pierce

Illustrations by
Dennis Hockerman

$\mathcal{E}$mma, a humble country mouse, beamed with pride at her vegetable garden. The radishes, potatoes, carrots, and beans were in full bloom.

"What a spectacular garden I have this year," she exclaimed. "I must invite my cousin Henry from the city to join me for a grand harvest feast."

Emma went into her snug home beneath the roots of an old oak tree. She sat down at her desk and wrote her cousin a letter.

A week later, there was a knock at the door. "Hello, cousin!" said Henry with a big smile. "Thanks ever so much for inviting me. It's nice to be away from all the *hububbity-bub-bub* of the city."

"I'm so happy to see you, Henry," Emma said. "I hope you brought a big appetite with you."

"That I did. But that's not all. I also brought you a present." Henry handed Emma a large gift.

"Oh, how wonderful!" Emma twittered with excitement. She ripped off the wrapping paper and stared at her gift. "What is it, Henry?"

"A back scratcher," Henry declared. He grabbed it and started scratching his back. "Clever, huh?"

"Thank you, Henry. You city mice have all sorts of marvelous things I can't even imagine," said Emma.

"You must be hungry after your journey," Emma said. "Dinner's coming right up."

"My four favorite words," said Henry, licking his lips.

Emma set down large steaming bowls of freshly cooked vegetables on the table. The two mice cousins enjoyed a delicious meal.

"Your fresh vegetables and clear country air make me as happy as a mouse in a cheese shop," Henry said.

"Thank you, Emma," said Henry. "That was a splendid meal. Now, what's for dessert?"

"Dessert? Oh, no!" Emma exclaimed. "I meant to pick a big basket of fresh berries, but then I started cooking and forgot all about dessert." Emma looked around her kitchen frantically for something to serve. She spied a parsnip and picked it up. "Henry, dear, wouldn't you like some parsnips for dessert?" she asked hopefully.

"Parsnips," Henry laughed, "are not for dessert. Why don't I run to the corner store and get us something sweet?"

"The *what*?" Emma gazed at him curiously.

"The corner store. Don't tell me you don't have a corner store?"

"No, cousin," Emma giggled. "Here in the country we grow all our food."

"I thought gardening was just a hobby," said Henry. "Grow your own food? I couldn't do that. The only thing I would grow is *hungry*."

"I should have brought something from the city," said Henry. "We have the most wonderful desserts you've ever tasted." Henry jumped up. "I know. Why don't you come with me into the city for dessert?"

"Really?" Emma asked.

"Really," Henry replied.

"Wait just a minute while I get my hat," Emma said, and the two mice set off for the city.

When the two travelers reached the city, Emma looked around at all the amazing sights. The buildings were so tall they blocked the sky from view. Cars and trucks raced about blaring their horns. People were in a terrific rush.

"What a busy place the city is," Emma remarked.

"Yes, isn't it great?" Henry said. "It's always busy. Hang on tight, we're almost there." Henry drove down crowded streets and alleys until they came to a three-story townhouse.

"This is my home, cousin," Henry said.

"Oh, Henry, it's glorious." Emma was enchanted by the look of his stately building. "And that," Henry pointed to the restaurant, "is where we'll get our dessert. It's called Sweet Treats. No one is there now because it is so late. Let's go."

SWEET TREATS

CLOSED

Emma and Henry scurried under the front
door of Sweet Treats and ran to the kitchen.

"Dessert!" Henry said, pointing to the cart
that towered over them.

They ran up the tablecloth and onto the
dessert cart.

The cart was filled with the most colorful, fancy foods Emma had ever seen. There were layer cakes, pink-frosted cakes, cupcakes, chocolate éclairs, cheesecakes and pies of all kinds.

"There," Henry declared. "That was worth the climb, wasn't it?"

Emma nodded, amazed and out of breath.

"Don't just look, cousin — eat, eat, eat away!" Henry dug into a cheesecake decorated with raspberries. Emma scooped out a chunk of layer cake and nibbled. She had never experienced anything like this before. She was dizzy with delight.

"Oh, my," she said.

"I told you," Henry smiled. "The city is the best!"

Suddenly, they heard a loud *"Meeeeeeow!"*

"What was that?" Emma nearly leaped out of her mouse fur.

"That's the cook's cat, Pierre. We'd better run before he catches us in here."

They scrambled down to the floor, but there was Pierre — waiting for them with sharp claws and bared teeth.

"*Run!*" yelled Henry. Pierre swiped a paw at them as they dove under the stove.

"The back door!" Henry gasped for breath. "We have to make a run for it."

"Ready when you are, cousin." Emma and Henry dashed out from under the stove. But Pierre flew through the air. His paw landed on Emma's tail. She was trapped.

"Help!" cried Emma.

Emma looked up into the big, glowing eyes of the cat. Slyly the cat smiled as he raised one paw over Emma's head. Suddenly, Henry leaped through the air, grabbing onto the cat's whiskers and began swinging back and forth.

Pierre yowled. He lifted his paw to swipe at the little mouse who was causing him such great pain — and Emma was free!

Henry let go of Pierre's whiskers at just the right time and slid across the kitchen floor, under the back door and into the backyard. Emma scampered out right behind him.

"Follow me under the fence," Henry said. "Once we get across the yard, we're home."

In the yard, Henry whispered, "*Shhhh*," as he pointed to a large snoring dog, sleeping in his doghouse. "That's Rufus. He doesn't like mice." Slowly they tiptoed past Rufus, trying not to wake him. But Rufus opened his eyes and spied Emma and Henry.

"*RRRRGH*," Rufus growled at them.

"Come on, cousin. *Hurry!*" Henry said. The
two mice dashed to the house as Rufus bounded
after them.

Once inside, Emma and Henry stopped to catch their breath. "Finally," Henry said, "we're home."

Emma collapsed into the first chair she could find and let out a big sigh of relief.

Henry smiled and said, "So, wasn't that the most heavenly dessert you ever tasted?"

"Yes, cousin, it was. But are you sure it was worth all that danger? I don't think I'll ever get to sleep tonight after all that excitement."

"I'll get you a cup of tea," Henry said. "That will help you settle down."

"Henry," Emma said as she drank her tea, "the city life is exciting, but it isn't for me. I prefer the country where a mouse can eat in peace."

"I understand," Henry said. "The city is not for everyone, but I love it."

"And I love the country. Do promise me, dear Henry," Emma said taking him by the paw, "that you will come to my house next autumn when my vegetables are once again tall and beautiful."

"Of course I will, Emma. And next time, I'll bring the dessert! Now, I'll take you home."

The next evening while cousin Henry went out for a night of dancing in the big city, Emma settled in for a homemade meal of turnip and cabbage stew, followed by a nice quiet cup of tea. "Ah," she sighed, "there's nothing like the country."